THAT TRICKY COYOTE!

Other Books by Gretchen Will Mayo

Meet Tricky Coyote

Earthmaker's Tales
North American Indian Stories About Earth Happenings

Star Tales
North American Indian Stories About the Stars

Books Illustrated by Gretchen Will Mayo

Whale Brother

THAT TRICKY COYOTE!

Retold and Illustrated by
Gretchen Will Mayo

WALKER AND COMPANY **NEW YORK**

PEOPLE IMAGINE COYOTE IN MANY WAYS. SOME SAY COYOTE SHIMMERS. THIS IS THE VISION THAT GREW IN THE ARTIST'S MIND AS SHE GOT TO KNOW COYOTE AND DREW THE PICTURES FOR THIS BOOK.

First published in the United States of America in 1993 by Walker Publishing Company, Inc.
Published simultaneously in Canada by Thomas Allen & Son Canada, Limited, Markham, Ontario

Library of Congress Cataloging-in-Publication Data
Mayo, Gretchen.
That tricky Coyote! / retold by Gretchen Will Mayo.
p.   cm.
Includes bibliographical references (p.   ).
Summary: A collection of legends about the cunning trickster Coyote, taken from a variety of Native American sources.
ISBN 0-8027-8200-0 (cloth). —ISBN 0-8027-8201-9 (reinforced)
1. Coyote (Legendary character).   2. Indians of North America—Legends.   [1. Coyote (Legendary character)   2. Indians of North America—Legends.]   I. Title.
E98.F6M36   1993
398.24'52974442—dc20   92-12440
CIP
AC

The art was prepared in opaque acrylic paints on paper.

Book Design by Georg Brewer

Printed in Hong Kong
10 9 8 7 6 5 4 3 2 1

For the McCowns, Paulie, Bill, Alex, Andrew, and Hillary
—Friends who became family.

CONTENTS

ACKNOWLEDGMENTS

In researching the Coyote stories and pictures, I was helped by many people and institutions. I offer thanks and admiration to Dr. Jay Miller, D'Arcy McNickle Center for the History of the American Indian, The Newberry Library, Chicago; the Milwaukee Public Museum and its library staff (especially Judy Turner); the State Historical Society of Colorado; the Marquette University Library Archives Department; the University of Wisconsin for use of its library; Joseph Bruchac, Abenaki storyteller and author; Dr. Kimberly Blaeser; and Dr. Alice B. Kehoe, anthropologist and author of *North American Indians: A Comprehensive Account*, Prentice-Hall, Inc., 1981.

I am indebted to Margaret Jensen, who read the manuscript in progress, for sharing her enthusiasm for and expertise in books for the early reader.

THAT TRICKY COYOTE!

Look out!
Here comes that rascal Coyote.
What a fast talker!
Coyote says, "I can do anything I want!"
He brought us fire,
made the seasons,
and tossed the sun into the sky.

But does Coyote want to behave?
No way!
Is he nosy?
You bet!
Is he lazy?
Does he brag?
All the time!

When will you learn, Coyote?

Boo! Coyote

Coyote was walking along. He climbed a high hill. At the top he looked down, down and saw a lake. How it sparkled in the sun! Coyote sat on a rock to rest and watch.

Splish! Splash! Down in the lake, fish jumped for bugs.

Splish! Splash! There were lots of bugs. There were lots of hungry fish.

Coyote licked his mouth. "I'm hungry, too!" he said. "But no bugs for me! I want fish to eat!"

Coyote went down, down the hill. Shish-shish-shish-shish, he walked through the tall grass. Whoosh, whoosh, whoosh, he ran across the sand and looked. All over the lake, fish jumped for bugs.

"So many good fish!" laughed Coyote. He looked down into the lake for fish.

But instead of fish, Coyote saw his own face in the water.

Coyote jumped back. Way back!

"Help!" yelled Coyote. "An ugly monster is hiding in the water! Help! Help!"

Whoosh! He ran back across the sand. Shish! He ran through the tall grass. Zip! He hid behind a rock. Was the ugly monster coming, too? Coyote peeked back down at the lake. No one was chasing Coyote. No ugly, drippy monster was coming.

All Coyote saw was Antelope. Antelope walked through the tall grass. She walked across the sand to the lake. Antelope bent her head down and took a long drink of water from the lake. Then she slowly walked away.

"Why isn't Antelope afraid?" thought Coyote. "Why didn't she run away? Maybe the monster is gone. I will find out!"

Zip! Coyote ran around the rock. Shish-shish-shish-shish, he ran through the tall grass. Whoosh, whoosh, whoosh, he ran across the sand to the lake. Coyote looked in the water and saw his own face again.

"Help!" yelled Coyote as he jumped way back. "The ugly monster is back!"

Coyote started to run. But then he heard a voice.

"Who is making all that noise?" croaked the voice.

"Oh no! Now the monster is yelling at me," cried Coyote. "And his voice is ugly, too!"

"I'm no monster. I'm a frog!" croaked the voice. Frog jumped over to the sand.

Coyote came back. He looked right at Frog. "Why did you scare me like that, Frog?" shouted Coyote. "You sound so ugly. You look so ugly, too."

Frog frowned. "Listen, Coyote!" he said. "If you don't like my looks, close your eyes."

"Good idea," said Coyote. He closed his eyes tight. Then Coyote bent down and took a long drink of water. Nothing chased him. Nobody grabbed him.

"How about that!" laughed Coyote with his eyes shut tight. "This time there was no monster. Good for me! I scared that monster away!"

"Boo! Coyote" is from a story told by John Duncan, a Ute from White Rock, Utah; it was recorded in 1909. Early people of the Ute nation, living in the Rocky Mountain areas, called themselves The People of the Shining Mountains.

THE SKY IS FALLING!

Coyote was walking along under the hot sun. He stopped to admire a tall, yellow sunflower. Then Coyote saw Lizard on the sunflower stalk. "Just what I need! A nice, fat lizard for lunch!" laughed Coyote, and he opened his mouth wide. Coyote was just about to take a big bite when clever Lizard saw him.

"Stop!" Lizard cried. "Don't move! Can't you see I'm very, very busy?"

"Seems to me you're just sitting there, waiting to be my lunch," Coyote answered.

"Wrong!" cried Lizard. "I'm holding up this sunflower stalk. And the sunflower is holding up the sky."

Coyote looked up, up at the sunflower. It reached high above him. It reached right up to the sky.

Then Coyote's stomach growled. Rrrrrr! Grrrrrr! Coyote looked back down at Lizard. "So what!" said Coyote. "Who cares about the sunflower? I want lunch!" And he opened his mouth wide again.

"Wait!" Lizard cried. "If I let go of this sunflower, the sky will fall."

Just then a puff of wind blew past. The sunflower shook and shivered.

"See! What did I tell you!" yelled Lizard. "The sky is so heavy and I am so tired. Please help me, Coyote. Help me hold the sunflower so the sunflower can hold up the sky."

Coyote looked up again. Clouds moved like giant white buffalos across the big, blue sky. Coyote felt dizzy watching them.

"Oh, no! Don't let that big sky fall on me!" shouted Coyote. He grabbed the sunflower stalk. He held tight so it would not move.

"The sky is so big, and we are so small," said Coyote, holding tight.

"Yes, yes!" answered Lizard. "We need help. I will get my children. They can help us hold the sunflower, so the sunflower can hold up the sky."

"Good idea!" answered Coyote.

"Don't let go," Lizard said. "Hang on until I come back with my children." Lizard slithered down the sunflower stalk. "Hee hee hee!" she laughed. Then Lizard zipped under some rocks and was gone.

Coyote hung on to the sunflower. "All this work makes me

hungry," sighed Coyote. "Where is Lizard? Where are her tasty children?"

The sun made the ground hot. It burned Coyote's back. Still, he held on so the sky would not fall.

"Lizard! Lizard! Come back!" shouted Coyote. "I'm so hungry. I'm so hot!"

But Lizard didn't hear.

Lizard, that fast thinker, was safe beneath the rocks. She was taking a nap with her children.

Tricky Coyote finds himself tricked into holding up the sky in related stories from the Hopi, Apache, and Ute nations, all located in the southwest. "The Sky Is Falling!" is adapted from several renditions of an old Apache tale. The people we know as Apache called themselves Dineh, *their word for "the people."* Dineh *is a name they much prefer to Apache, which came from the Zuni word* apachu, *meaning "the enemy."*

Where Is My Song?

Coyote was walking along when he heard a noise. "Who is that singing?" he cried. He looked down. He looked up. How about that! There was Cicada, sitting on the branch of a crooked piñon tree.

"I like your song," Coyote called to Cicada. "Will you teach it to me? Then I can take it home and sing it for my family."

"Sure!" said Cicada. And Cicada sang his song again.

"Now let me try!" cried Coyote. Coyote lifted his voice and howled, "Whoooooooo!"

"Have I got it?" Coyote asked as he finished.

"Well, sort of," answered Cicada.

"Sort of isn't good enough," said Coyote. "Let me try once more. I want my song to be just right." So Coyote lifted his voice and howled even louder. "Wa wa wooooooo!"

"Stop!" Cicada cried. "Save your voice for your family."

"Good idea!" said Coyote. And he ran off to take his song home.

Coyote ran fast. He ran so fast that he didn't see Mole's hole. Flump! Bump! Bump! Coyote rolled over and over and over. He rubbed the dust from his eyes and sat up.

"Oh, no!" Coyote cried. "Where is my song? I forgot my song!" So Coyote ran all the way back to the piñon tree. Cicada was still there.

"Good thing you're here," Coyote called to Cicada. "I fell in Mole's hole. I fell so hard that I lost my song. Will you teach me again?"

Cicada answered, "I'll teach you once more. But only if you will be more careful this time."

"I will! I will!" promised Coyote.

So Cicada sang his song for Coyote. Coyote sang, too. "Wa wa wooooooo!" His singing was very loud.

When he finished trying out the song, Coyote promised, "I'll be careful. I'll watch for the mole hole." And then he left.

Coyote did not run too fast. He watched the ground for Mole's hole. He watched the ground and ran along. He watched the ground and . . . ran right into a bush.

Tweee, twee, twee, twee! A crowd of birds flew out of the bush. They zipped and whistled around Coyote's head.

"Hey! Stop that noise!" cried Coyote. He covered his ears. He closed his eyes. But the noise filled his head.

Coyote forgot his song again.

This time Cicada saw Coyote walking back to the piñon tree. Cicada thought, "That Coyote! He sings too loud. He always forgets. What a pest! I think I will teach Coyote a lesson!"

So Cicada took off his coat. He stuffed it with stones and mud. Then he left his coat in the piñon tree and he flew away.

Coyote marched right to the piñon tree. He saw Cicada's stiff old clothes sitting up there. But Coyote thought he saw Cicada. "Cicada, I'm glad you're still here!" called Coyote. "A bunch of birds took the song out of my head. Could you sing it again?"

Cicada's stiff old coat didn't answer.

"Cicada! Answer me!" said Coyote. "I lost my song. Sing it again!"

Cicada's coat didn't sing.

"Cicada!" Coyote yelled. "If you don't sing, I will eat you." Four times Coyote shouted his warning. Four times Coyote said, "I will eat you!"

But Cicada's coat didn't sing.

So, snap! Coyote's sharp teeth grabbed Cicada's clothes.

Chomp! Coyote bit the mud and stones.

"Owwwwwww! That smarts!" cried Coyote. He held his jaw and cried, "Ow! Ow! Owwwwwww!"

Far away, Cicada heard Coyote. "Listen to that," said Cicada. "Coyote finally remembered the song."

Long ago a Zuni storyteller watched a cicada (often called "locust" by white settlers and recorders) shed its nymph skin to emerge as an adult. The storyteller made the cicada a character in a favorite Coyote story. "Where Is My Song?" is based on a version of that tale told by Tsatiselu in about 1917 when she was 80 years old. There are many similar stories about forgetful Coyote told by the Zunis and other people today. The Zuni pueblo is located in New Mexico.

BLUE COYOTE

Coyote was walking along and watching Bluebird.

"You are the most beautiful bird in the sky. I wish I were blue like you," Coyote called to Bluebird.

"Coyotes aren't blue," laughed Bluebird.

"Maybe they should be," answered Coyote. "What makes you blue?"

"I wash in the blue lake," said Bluebird.

16

"Anything else?" Coyote asked.

"When I wash in the blue lake I sing this song:

     I am blue as the water.

     I am blue as the water."

"But, I'm afraid to jump in the lake. I don't like to be wet," Coyote said.

"Then you will never be blue," Bluebird answered.

"Okay, Okay! I'll try the blue lake," said Coyote. Coyote went to the water and jumped in. "Brrrrrr!!" shivered Coyote. "I don't like to be wet. I don't like to be cold."

Scrub, scrub, scrub. Coyote washed in the blue lake.

"I am blue as the water. I am blue as the water," howled Coyote. He made a terrible noise. When he came out, he was still Coyote color.

"Hey! I'm not blue," yelled Coyote to Bluebird.

"Wash some more," Bluebird answered. "I washed four times."

"So many times! Do I *have* to?" cried Coyote.

"Do you want to be blue?" asked Bluebird.

Coyote answered, "Yes, yes! I want to be blue just like you!"

So Coyote washed and sang and sang and washed three more times.

"That was awful!" Coyote said when he came out. His teeth were chattering. His legs were shaking. "I'm freezing! But look, Bluebird! At last I'm blue!" cried Coyote.

"Good thing," said Bluebird. "Your singing is terrible."

"Look how beautiful I am," laughed Coyote. He turned around and around. Coyote was so proud. He wanted everyone to see how beautiful he was.

"See how beautiful I am," he called to Rabbit.

"Don't you wish you were beautiful, too?" he cried to Deer.

Coyote looked behind. "See, even my shadow is blue!" Coyote looked and looked at his blue shadow. He did not look where he was going.

Crash! Flip! Flop! Coyote bumped into a rock. He rolled over and over in the dirt. Now he wasn't blue anymore. Coyote was dirt brown.

"Oh, no! Now I'm an old dusty color," cried Coyote.

"Jump in the lake and sing again," Bluebird called.

"No way! I don't like to be wet. I don't want to be cold." Coyote complained. "I'll stay this way."

"Good thing," Bluebird said to herself. "Coyote's singing is terrible."

Now Coyote says, "It's Bluebird's fault that all Coyotes are dusty brown instead of blue."

Jose Lewis was a highly respected O'odham scholar who recorded stories and wrote reports for the Smithsonian Institution. "Blue Coyote" is retold from one of the O'odham stories Jose Lewis recorded in 1904. The O'odham people were once called Pima Indians. Their traditional homeland is in the place we now call Arizona.

I Win!

Coyote was walking along when he saw Turtle.

"You look tired," Coyote said to Turtle. "Why are you resting?"

Turtle answered, "Because I was just in the big race."

"Race? What race?" Coyote asked.

Turtle looked surprised. "The Big Turtle Race. Haven't you heard? All the turtles had a race down along the river."

"Who won?" asked Coyote.

"I did!" answered Turtle. "And guess what! I've never lost a turtle race. I'm the Turtle Race champ!"

"Well, I've never lost a race either," said Coyote. "That makes me a champ, too!"

Turtle shook his head. "There can't be two champs. I'm the one and only racing champ!"

"No, no, no," cried Coyote. "I'm bigger. I'm faster."

Turtle said, "Yes, yes, Coyote. You always say you are the best. Some day we will race and find out."

"You're on!" said Coyote. "We will race tomorrow. I will be the champ!" And then Coyote left.

Turtle watched Coyote walk away and thought, "What have I done? Why did I brag? Now I have to race Coyote."

So Turtle called together all the other turtles. He told them about the race with Coyote. He said, "I'm sorry that I bragged."

"That tricky Coyote!" cried Grandfather Turtle. "Why doesn't he let us turtles alone!"

"Coyote is big. Coyote is fast. Coyote will be the winner!" said Turtle.

"Maybe not," said Grandfather Turtle. "Turtles are small.

Turtles are slow. But there are more of us. Maybe a lot of small, slow turtles can trick one big, fast Coyote."

"Yes! Yes!" everyone shouted. "But how?"

"All of us will race Coyote," answered Grandfather Turtle. "But we will race one at a time. And we will each race for just a little while." Grandfather Turtle gave a white feather to each turtle. He told them to wear the feather for the race. Then Grandfather Turtle showed everyone what to do.

The next day Coyote and Turtle lined up to race.

"Here I am, the Turtle Race champ!" called Coyote.

"Not yet," said Turtle. He was wearing his white feather.

"One, two, three, go!" shouted Grandfather Turtle. And the race began.

Coyote started, but not too fast. He thought, "Turtle is so

slow. He will creep along. I can take it easy." So Coyote took it easy all the way to the first turn in the path. But when he made the first turn, Coyote could not believe what he saw. There was a turtle with a white feather running ahead. The turtle was running as fast as he could. Wiggle, waggle, wiggle, waggle.

"How did Turtle get here so fast?" Coyote wondered. "I will have to run faster." So Coyote passed the turtle with the white feather. "Eat my dust!" Coyote yelled to the turtle.

Coyote dashed around the second turn. And Coyote had a second surprise. There was a turtle with a white feather running in front of him. Wiggle, waggle, wiggle, waggle.

Coyote thought, "Turtle caught up with me again! I can't take it easy. I can't slow down. I will race as fast as I can."

Coyote rushed ahead. He shot to the next turn. Puff, puff! But when Coyote made the turn, there was a turtle with the white feather again. "Turtle keeps passing me! He keeps passing with his white feather," puffed Coyote.

There were lots of turns on the racing path. There were lots of turtles with white feathers. Coyote raced faster and faster.

"Puff, puff, puff!" Coyote was out of breath. "Puff, puff, puff!" Coyote's legs felt like they were melting. "I can't take another step!" cried Coyote. Then Coyote dropped on the path. He dropped just like a falling tree. Coyote lay there on the path, puff, puff, puffing.

Then Turtle came along. Wiggle, waggle. He ran with his white feather right past puffing Coyote. Turtle raced down the path and crossed the finish line all alone.

"I win!" shouted Turtle.

"No, *we* win," said Grandfather Turtle.

"I'll never race a turtle again," puffed Coyote.

In about 1904, a Caddoan storyteller named Wing told a popular tale about a race between Coyote and Turtle. "I Win!" is adapted from his story and similar versions told by the Arikara Indians of South Dakota. Most of the Caddo Indians live in Oklahoma today but their ancestors lived in the area where Arkansas, Louisiana, and Texas meet. The Caddoan language is also spoken by the Arikara, but they are more closely related to the Pawnee.

WHO IS COYOTE?

While it can become overly romanticized, Indians do favor circles over squares and webs over grids. The world of the Indian has a roundness and a closeness that reflect important values. Within every circle there is a center that holds everything together. For the village, the center was usually the community hall or the house of the leader. On tribal lands, the center was often a sacred mountain, spring, or special place. In the stories of Native American tribes living in Western North America, Coyote became another such center.

Coyote was a complex character who stood at the center of many things. Because he was at the very middle, Coyote could see and do anything in any direction, whether it was for good or bad, to hurt or to help. Some stories have Coyote holding up the sky or changing the temperament of an entire species of animal. Often hills and trees are located where they are because of something Coyote did or did not do that changed the world forever.

29

Coyote was so important you would think that he knew how to behave, or would at least learn. But as you see, he did not. As often as not, Coyote set a bad example and sometimes a horrible one. Only too rarely, he managed to do something nice, although this was almost never by deliberate design. Even so, people act the way they do now because of something that Coyote did during the time that the world was forming.

In this way Coyote was and is a fixture of the life and landscape of Native America. While other parts of the Americas had other animals who served a similar role, such as Rabbit in the East and Raven along the coasts of the northern Pacific, only Coyote was truly an American original. Coyote owes his importance both to the wily ways of a real coyote and to the intimate ties that humans and canines have had for eons. What makes Coyote so distinctly American, moreover, is the manner in which this character is cast in these stories.

Gretchen Will Mayo has taken care to tailor her selections to a young audience and has wisely limited the panoramic perspective that got Coyote into so much trouble over the generations. Here he is wise and foolish and childish, but nevertheless entertaining. He lives as much in the world of today as in the world of our ancestors. Coyote's stories teach us the importance of sustaining the diversity of life on earth for the benefit of the global community in which Coyote is both first citizen and last resort.

Jay Miller, Ph.D.,
D'Arcy McNickle Center for the History of the American Indian,
The Newberry Library, Chicago

SOURCES

U sually scholars in the fields of anthropology and ethnology were the first to record tales told by American Indian storytellers. It should always be remembered, however, that the stories belong to the creative Indians who told them. We thank and honor those Native Americans who shared their stories for the following reporters and publications:

Dorsey, George A., Ph.D. *Traditions of the Skidi Pawnee*. Memoirs of the American Folklore Society, vol. 8. Boston: Houghton, Mifflin and Company, 1904.

Traditions of the Arikara. Publication of the Carnegie Institution, vol. 27. Washington, D.C., 1904.

Traditions of the Caddo. Publication of the Carnegie Institution, vol. 41. Washington,D.C., 1905.

Mason, J. Alden. "Myths of the Uintah Utes." *Journal of American Folklore* 23: 299–363.

Parsons, Elsie Clews. "Pueblo-Indian Folktales, Probably of

Spanish Provenance." *Journal of American Folklore* 31: 216–55.

Russell, Frank. *The Pima Indians.* 26th Annual Report to the Bureau of American Ethnology, Washington, D.C., 1904–5.

Voth, H. R. *Traditions of the Hopi.* The Stanley McCormick Hopi Expedition, Field Columbian Museum Publication #96, vol. 8. Chicago, 1905.

These additional resources were used for background information:

Coffer, William. *Where Is the Eagle?* New York: Van Nostrand Reinhold and Company, 1981.

Fontana, Bernard L. *Introduction* to the 2d edition of *The Pima Indians* by Frank Russell. Tucson: University of Arizona Press, 1975.

Lopez, Barry Holstun. *Giving Birth to Thunder, Sleeping with His Daughter.* New York: Avon Books, 1977.

Miller, Jay. Introduction and Notes to *Coyote Stories.* Lincoln: University of Nebraska Press, First Bison Book Printing, 1990.

Mourning Dove. *Coyote Stories.* Lincoln: University of Nebraska Press, First Bison Book Printing, 1990.

Opler, Morris Edward. *Myths and Tales of the Jicarilla Apache Indians*. Memoirs of the American Folklore Society, vol. 31. New York: J. J. Augustin, 1938.

———.*Myths and Legends of the Lipan Apache Indians*. Memoirs of the American Folklore Society, vol. 36. New York: J. J. Augustin, 1940.

Parsons, Elsie Clews. *Tewa Tales*. Memoirs of the American Folklore Society, vol. 19. Boston and New York: Houghton, Mifflin and Company, 1926.

———.*Taos Tales*. Memoirs of the American Folklore Society, vol. 34. New York: J. J. Augustin, 1940.

Radin, Paul. *The Trickster, A Study in American Indian Mythology*. London: Routledge and Kegan Paul, 1956.

Tedlock, Barbara. *The Clown's Way—Teachings from the American Earth*. New York: Liveright Press, 1975.

Tedlock, Dennis. *The Spoken Word and the Work of Interpretation*. Philadelphia: University of Pennsylvania Press, 1983.